Creature Features

Anita Ganeri • Illustrated by Steve Fricker

Simon & Schuster Books for Young Readers

SIMON & SCHUSTER BOOKS FOR YOUNG READERS
An imprint of Simon & Schuster Children's Publishing Division
1230 Avenue of the Americas, New York, New York 10020

SIMON & SCHUSTER BOOKS FOR YOUNG READERS
is a trademark of Simon & Schuster.

This book was conceived, edited, and designed by
Marshall Editions
170 Piccadilly, London W1V 9DD

First American Edition, 1997

Printed and bound in Italy by Officine Grafiche de Agostini, Novara
Originated in Singapore by Master Image

10 9 8 7 6 5 4 3 2 1

Library of Congress Cataloging-in-Publication Data

Ganeri, Anita, 1961-
        Creature Features / Anita Ganeri ; illustrated by Steve Fricker.
                p.   cm. — (How it works)
        Includes index.
        Summary: Describes animals and how their bodies work, focusing on animals with
unusual characteristics.
        ISBN 0-689-81186-1
        1. Animals—Miscellanea—Juvenile literature. 2. Animals—Physiology—
Miscellanea—Juvenile literature. 3. Animals—Anatomy—Miscellanea—Juvenile
literature. [1. Animals—Miscellanea. 2. Animals—Physiology.] I. Fricker, Steve, ill.
II. Title. III. Series: How it works (Simon & Schuster Books for Young Readers)
QL49.G2425
1997
591—dc20
96-38346
CIP
AC

Editor: Claire Berridge
Designers: Ian Winton, Steve Prosser
Managing Editor: Kate Phelps
Design Manager: Ralph Pitchford
Art Director: Branka Surla
Editorial Director: Cynthia O'Brien
Production: Janice Storr, Selby Sinton
Jacket Designer: Sandra Begnor
Researcher: Lynda Wargen

CONTENTS

ALL ABOUT ANIMALS

Animals are truly amazing! There are millions and millions of different kinds. They are divided into groups depending on how their beastly bits fit together. Animals with bones inside their bodies are called vertebrates (fish, amphibians, mammals, reptiles, and birds). Those without bones are known as invertebrates (crustaceans, arachnids, insects, and mollusks). Both of these big groups are divided into the smaller ones pictured here.

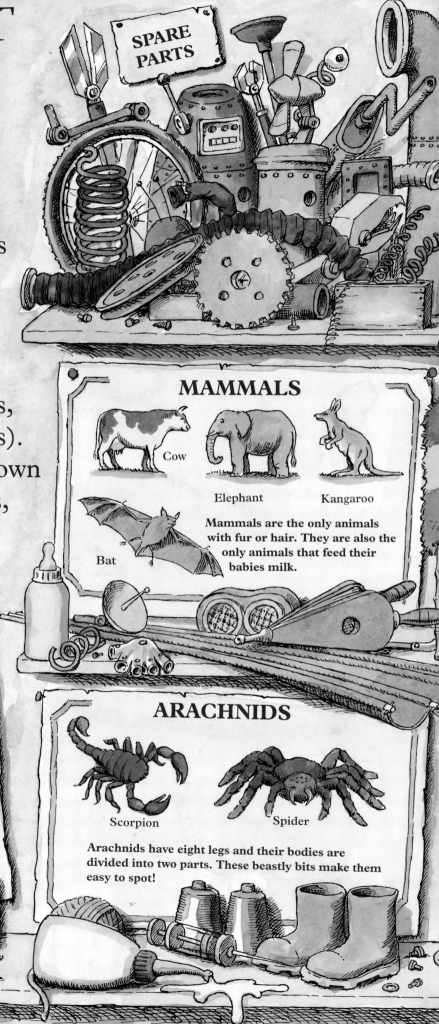

MAMMALS

Cow

Elephant

Kangaroo

Bat

Mammals are the only animals with fur or hair. They are also the only animals that feed their babies milk.

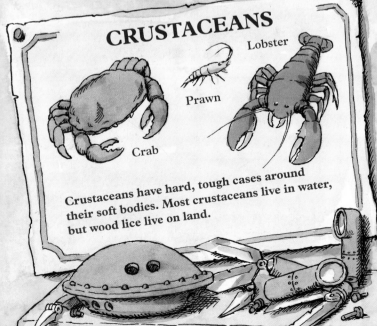

CRUSTACEANS

Lobster

Prawn

Crab

Crustaceans have hard, tough cases around their soft bodies. Most crustaceans live in water, but wood lice live on land.

ARACHNIDS

Scorpion

Spider

Arachnids have eight legs and their bodies are divided into two parts. These beastly bits make them easy to spot!

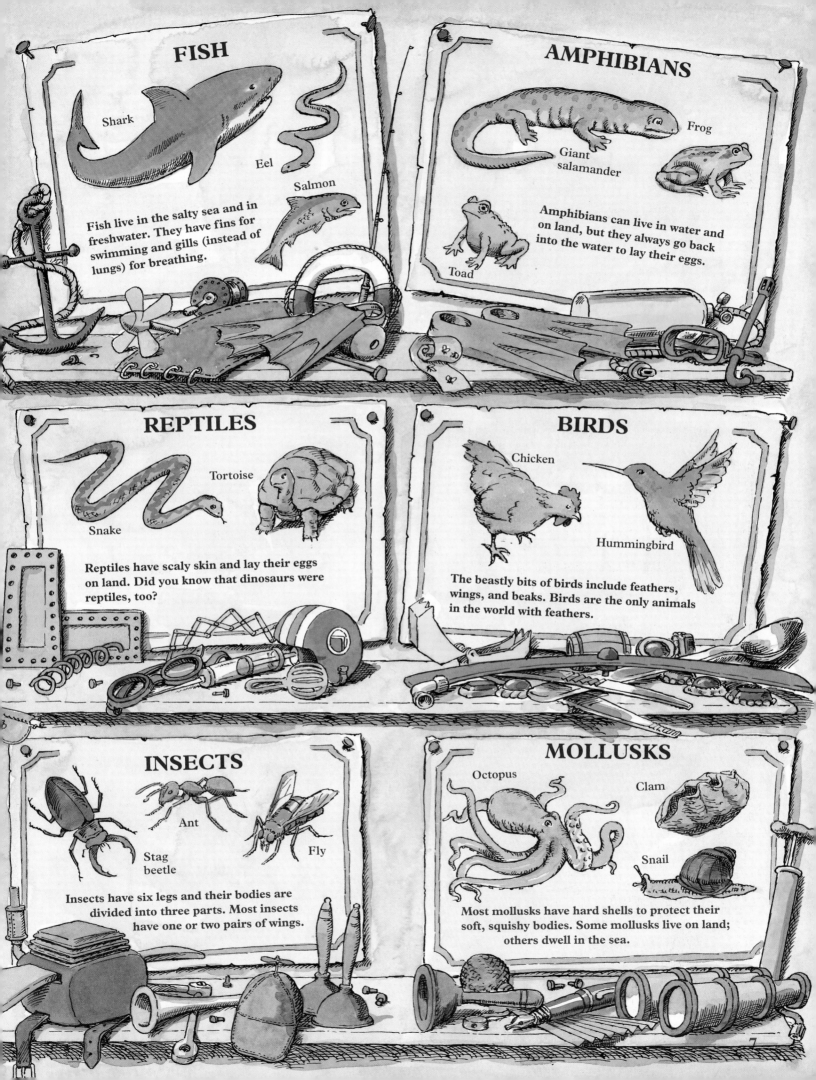

FISH

Shark

Eel

Salmon

Fish live in the salty sea and in freshwater. They have fins for swimming and gills (instead of lungs) for breathing.

AMPHIBIANS

Giant salamander

Frog

Toad

Amphibians can live in water and on land, but they always go back into the water to lay their eggs.

REPTILES

Snake

Tortoise

Reptiles have scaly skin and lay their eggs on land. Did you know that dinosaurs were reptiles, too?

BIRDS

Chicken

Hummingbird

The beastly bits of birds include feathers, wings, and beaks. Birds are the only animals in the world with feathers.

INSECTS

Ant

Stag beetle

Fly

Insects have six legs and their bodies are divided into three parts. Most insects have one or two pairs of wings.

MOLLUSKS

Octopus

Clam

Snail

Most mollusks have hard shells to protect their soft, squishy bodies. Some mollusks live on land; others dwell in the sea.

7

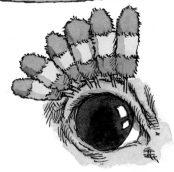

Next time you take a cool, refreshing sip of milk, spare a thought for the cow it came from. Each year cows give us millions of gallons of milk to drink or to make into yogurt and cheese. Now, to the beastly bits of cows!

Cows have very long eyelashes for brushing away pesky flies.

Furry ears keep out unwanted insects.

Cows have strong teeth for grinding up their food of grass and plants.

Horns

Eyelashes

Keep Out

Ear

Mouth and teeth

Stomach

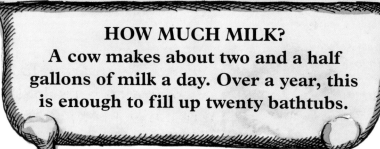

HOW MUCH MILK?
A cow makes about two and a half gallons of milk a day. Over a year, this is enough to fill up twenty bathtubs.

Hoof

The cow's hooves are like huge toenails that protect its feet.

A cow has four stomachs. When a cow eats grass, it grinds it up in its mouth and the goodness the grass contains is taken out. The first stomach makes the grass into little balls. These go back into the cow's mouth to be chewed again.

Udder

Horns First stomach: reticulum Third stomach: omasum

Food pipe

Second stomach: rumen Fourth stomach: abomasum Udder Tail Hoof

WHAT IS A COW?
Cows belong to the group of animals called mammals. They all make milk to feed their babies. Milk contains water and lots of nourishment, everything a baby needs to grow up big and strong.

The chewed grass passes through the other stomachs, and water and the good things in it are taken out and used to make milk.

The milk squirts out through udders on the cow's stomach. The udders are similar to the teats on a baby's bottle.

Tail

The cow's long, hairy tail makes a perfect flyswatter as it swishes from side to side.

Cowpat

Any waste from food digestion is pushed out to make a cowpat. *Splat!*

ALL ABOUT CHICKENS

How do you like your eggs? Boiled? Sunny-side up? Scrambled? Millions of eggs are eaten each year. Most come from chickens, scratching about in fields and farmyards. A chicken can lay an egg a day. But how does she do it? And which came first, the chicken or the egg?

When a chick is ready to hatch, a tiny tapping noise comes from its shell. The chick has a knobby bump on its beak. It uses this like a pick to chip away at the shell. Then it struggles out.

Beak

The chicken picks up corn quickly with its short, sharp beak—*peck! peck! peck!*

The raw materials for making an egg come from the corn and seeds the chicken eats.

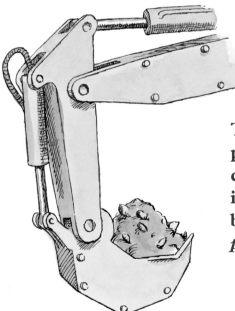

Claw

Chickens have digger-like claws for uncovering grains of corn, seeds, and . . . worms!

On its journey through the chicken, different parts are added to the egg. First comes the yolk, then the egg white, and finally the shell.

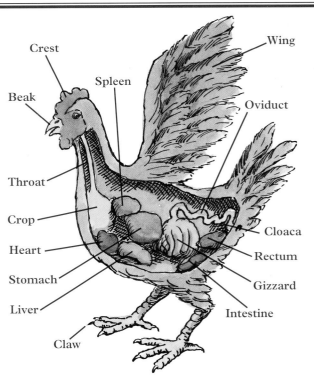

Crest
Beak
Throat
Crop
Heart
Stomach
Liver
Claw
Spleen
Wing
Oviduct
Cloaca
Rectum
Gizzard
Intestine

WHAT IS A CHICKEN?
A chicken is a type of bird. You can tell this by its feathers, wings, and beak. All birds lay hard-shelled eggs, which they keep warm and safe until they hatch.

The egg is ready to be laid! It is squeezed out of the chicken's body. This makes it oval-shaped instead of perfectly round.

Egg

Egg

Ostrich egg
Hummingbird egg
Chicken egg

RECORD BREAKERS!
The world's biggest bird lays the world's biggest eggs. A single ostrich egg weighs as much as twenty chicken eggs. Its shell is so strong that you can stand on it. The smallest and most delicate eggs are laid by tiny hummingbirds. They are barely as big as baked beans.

This snake is on the lookout for lunch. Many snakes use deadly poison to kill their food. They lie in wait until something strolls by, then raise their head, open their mouth wide, and . . . strike! As they bite, they inject poison into their prey. Then they swallow it whole.

A snake stores its poison in tiny tanks in its head. The poison trickles through tubes into the snake's fangs.

The snake's long, curved fangs are hollow teeth. They are needle sharp for injecting poison. Ouch!

A snake's skeleton is mostly made of backbone and ribs. This makes its body very long and bendy so that it can coil, twist, and slither.

Poison tank

Fang

Tongue

Skeleton

HOW DO SNAKES SMELL? With their tongues, that's how! They flick their forked tongues in and out, picking up smells from the air.

Eyes

Tail

You'll never outstare a snake! They can't blink because they don't have eyelids. Instead, they have see-through skin to protect their eyes.

Hinged jaw

To send a warning, a rattlesnake shakes the end of its tail. If this doesn't work, it bites!

A snake can open its mouth very wide to swallow food bigger than its head. This is because it has long, stretchy hinges between its jaws.

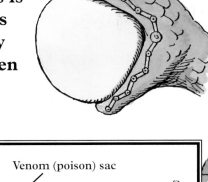

Some snakes wrap their coils around their dinner and squeeze it to death. They are called constrictors.

Venom opening

Venom (poison) sac

Scales

Fang

Rattle (tail)

Trachea

Jaw

Tongue

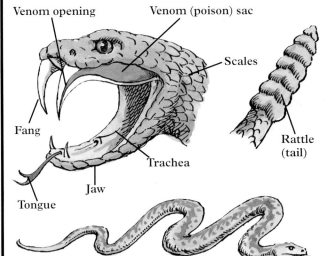

WHAT IS A SNAKE?

A snake is a reptile, an animal with scaly skin, related to lizards and alligators. The reticulated python is the longest snake. It can grow over thirty feet long. Tiger snakes are the deadliest snakes.

ALL ABOUT SPIDERS

If there's a spider about and you're a fly, watch out! Flies are a spider's favorite food. They catch them in sticky silk cobwebs. Some spiders spin webs between two twigs or blades of grass. Others use a dusty corner of your house! Then they sit and wait for a tasty fly to buzz by. . . .

Fly

A spider has eight tiny eyes.

Eyes

Fang

Feeler

The spider injects a fly with special juices. These turn the fly's insides into souplike mush so the spider can suck them out.

Flies stick to the gummy silk of the web. Spiders don't stick to their webs because their legs have oil on them.

The spider's mouth is armed with long, sharp fangs for grabbing its prey and injecting it with poison.

14

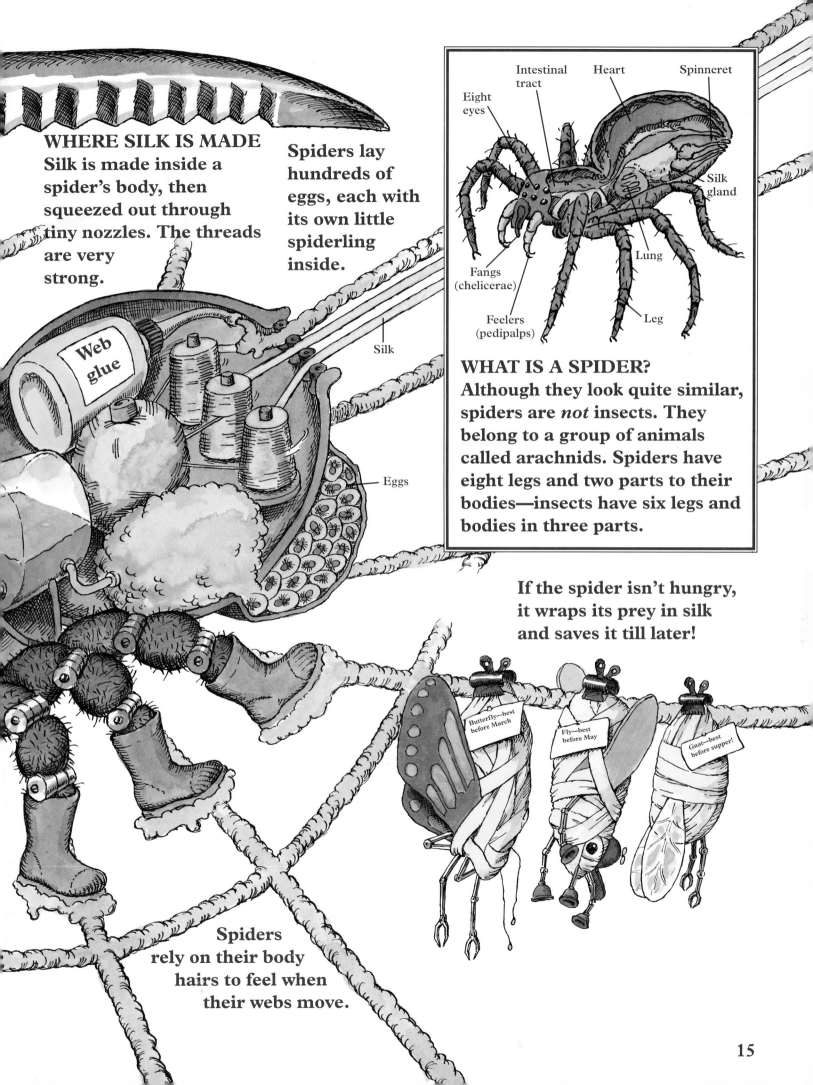

WHERE SILK IS MADE
Silk is made inside a spider's body, then squeezed out through tiny nozzles. The threads are very strong.

Spiders lay hundreds of eggs, each with its own little spiderling inside.

Web glue

Silk

Eggs

Intestinal tract

Heart

Spinneret

Eight eyes

Silk gland

Fangs (chelicerae)

Lung

Feelers (pedipalps)

Leg

WHAT IS A SPIDER?
Although they look quite similar, spiders are *not* insects. They belong to a group of animals called arachnids. Spiders have eight legs and two parts to their bodies—insects have six legs and bodies in three parts.

If the spider isn't hungry, it wraps its prey in silk and saves it till later!

Butterfly—best before March

Fly—best before May

Gnat—best before supper!

Spiders rely on their body hairs to feel when their webs move.

Kangaroos are built for bouncing. They bound along the ground on their long, strong back legs, using their tails for balance. Newborn baby kangaroos look nothing like their mothers. They are blind, hairless, and only as big as bees. They crawl into their mother's pouch and stay there for the next few months, drinking milk and growing bigger . . . and bouncier!

Kangaroos have large, twitching ears, like radar, for keeping track of what is going on around them.

Tail

Legs

A kangaroo uses its long tail to help keep its balance as it leaps. Otherwise, it would topple over. Its tail also props up the kangaroo when it is standing still.

In a group of kangaroos the biggest adult male is boss! Rival males fight with their front arms, sharp claws, and powerful back legs.

Ears

Front arms

Joey

Pouch

A kangaroo once leaped high enough to clear two cars, one on top of the other. It could have jumped right over you!

There are two types of milk for the joey (baby) to drink. Newborn joeys drink low-fat milk. Joeys that have left the pouch drink a high-fat blend.

Ears

Plantaris muscle

Tail

Forearms

Claws

Gastrocnemius muscle

Joey

Pouch

Heel

Toes

WHAT IS A KANGAROO?
A kangaroo is a type of animal called a marsupial. This means it is a mammal with a pouch for holding its baby. Kangaroos live only in Australasia.

ALL ABOUT ELEPHANTS

Everything about elephants is BIG! Their tusks, trunks, ears, and appetites! An elephant's trunk is in fact its nose. But it isn't just used for smelling. Elephants use their trunks for drinking, picking up food (and babies!), snorkeling, trumpeting, showering, and spraying on dust and mud to stop sunburn and insect bites.

HOW AN ELEPHANT USES ITS TRUNK

Snorkel

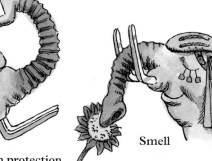

Shower

Sun protection

Smell

Ear

Eyelashes

Tusk

Trunk

Elephants use their tusks like forks for digging and lifting.

DID YOU KNOW?
Elephants can catch cold, just like you or me. Imagine the size of the hankie you'd need to blow your trunk!

18

African elephants have ears as big as bedsheets. They flap their ears to keep cool.

It takes a lot of breath for an elephant to suck up water through its trunk.

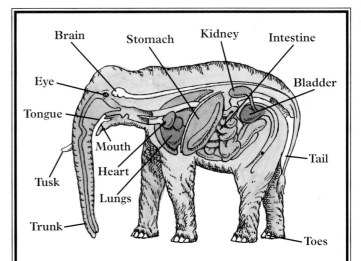

Brain Stomach Kidney Intestine

Eye

Tongue

Bladder

Mouth

Tusk

Heart

Lungs

Tail

Trunk

Toes

WHAT IS AN ELEPHANT?
The African elephant is the biggest animal on land, with the Asian elephant not far behind. African elephants have bigger ears and more toes on their feet than Asian elephants.

Lung

Rib

An elephant's ribs are so heavy they don't move when it breathes.

The elephant uses its long eyelashes and hairy tail to swat away irritating flies and ticks. *Whack!*

Tail

Leg

If the juiciest leaves are too high to reach, the elephant simply butts the tree with its head and pushes the whole thing over. Luckily, it has a hard head.

Elephants have huge legs like pillars. Their big, broad feet have soft soles to cushion their weight as they walk.

19

ALL ABOUT OCTOPUSES

There's no mistaking an octopus with its eight rubbery tentacles covered in suckers! Between each "arm" there is a web of skin that helps the octopus swim through the water when it is hunting for food. The octopus has another trick up its sleeves. It changes color to show its feelings and to hide from its hungry enemies.

An octopus has big, staring eyes and excellent eyesight for spotting things to eat.

Eye

Sucker

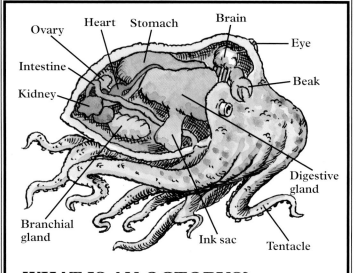

Ovary
Heart
Stomach
Brain
Eye
Intestine
Beak
Kidney
Digestive gland
Branchial gland
Ink sac
Tentacle

WHAT IS AN OCTOPUS?

An octopus is a mollusk related to mussels, oysters, snails, and squid. Unlike many mollusks, octopuses don't have shells.

HOW AN OCTOPUS SWIMS

The octopus sucks water into its body and then shoots it back out again. As the water jets out, it pushes the octopus backward. If it's escaping from enemies, the octopus also squirts out ink to cover its tracks.

Ink sac

Poison gland

The octopus has a parrotlike beak and a poisonous bite. It chews its food, then sucks it into its mouth.

An octopus can change its skin color

Tentacle

Pressure   Suction

The suckers work like tiny sink plungers. They give the octopus a very strong grip.

An octopus's tentacles are handy tools. They're good for catching food, crawling across the seabed, burrowing in the sand to hide, and building a nest.

ALL ABOUT TORTOISES

With its shiny, armor-plated shell, a tortoise is built like a miniature tank. The shell gives protection to the body, but it is hopeless for hurrying. Tortoises are serious slowpokes. They have such thick legs to support the great weight of their shells that they can't move very fast at all!

Tortoises don't have teeth. They grab and cut up food with their sharp, beaklike mouths, then gulp it down. They eat leaves and grass.

The hard bones of a tortoise's skull are like a crash helmet—they protect its head.

Shell

Skull

Mouth

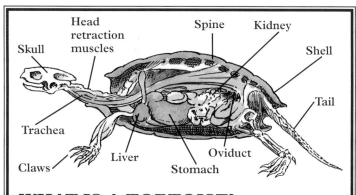

Head retraction muscles

Spine   Kidney

Skull

Shell

Trachea

Tail

Claws   Liver   Oviduct

Stomach

WHAT IS A TORTOISE?
Tortoises are reptiles. The first kind appeared on Earth about 200 million years ago. Tortoises are cold-blooded. They have to live in a warm place for their bodies to work properly.

A tortoise can pull its head, legs, and tail inside its shell for safety.

The tortoise's shell is made of plates of hard bone and horn. These are built up in three layers. The innermost layer is made of the tortoise's backbone and ribs. It forms the framework for the rest of the shell.

Tail

Rib

Foot

Leg joint

ALL ABOUT TURTLES
You can tell a turtle from a tortoise by its webbed feet and flipper legs. Turtles use these for swimming in the sea.

Turtle foot

Tortoise foot

Tortoises can live for more than seventy years. Some live twice that long! You can tell a tortoise's age by the number of growth rings on its shell.

The tortoise's tummy is protected by another plate of shell.

The biggest type of tortoise is the galapago giant tortoise. It can grow up to five feet long and can weigh up to 550 pounds. Some live for 200 years.

23

All About Bats

The bat's leathery wings stretch between its long, bony fingers and its legs.

Claw

Bats are strange-looking creatures with furry bodies and leathery wings. They sleep by day and come out at night to hunt for juicy moths to eat. Bats use sound to find their food. As they fly, they make very high squeaking sounds. The sounds hit an insect and send back an echo. The bat can find the insect from the echo.

Wing

Finger bone

Fruit bats sleep hanging upside down from a branch. They wrap up snugly in their leathery wings. Their back claws lock in place so they don't fall off!

The bat uses its hooklike thumbs for climbing, holding, and combing its fur.

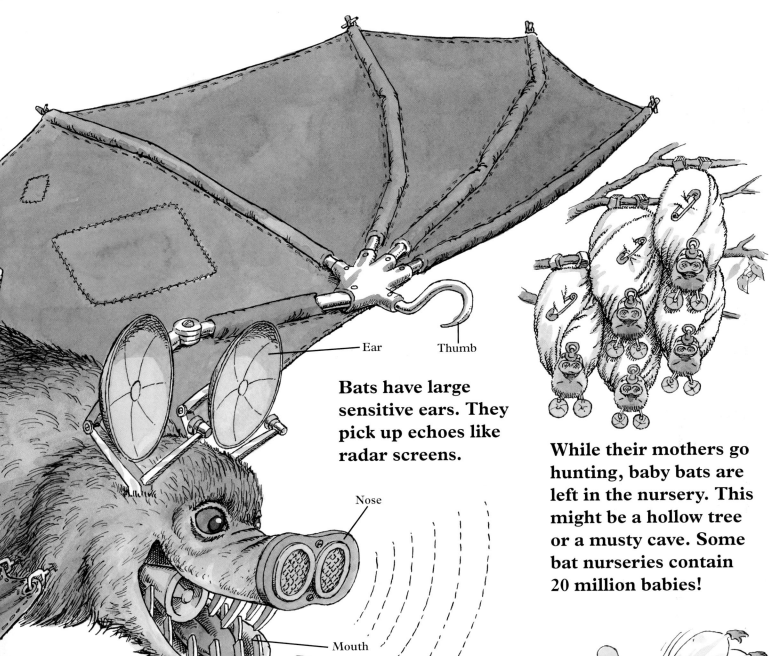

Ear   Thumb

Bats have large sensitive ears. They pick up echoes like radar screens.

Nose

Mouth

While their mothers go hunting, baby bats are left in the nursery. This might be a hollow tree or a musty cave. Some bat nurseries contain 20 million babies!

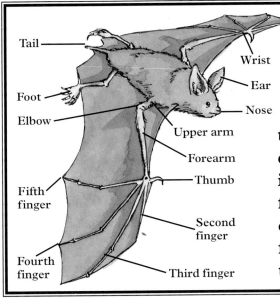

Tail

Foot

Elbow

Fifth finger

Fourth finger

Wrist

Ear

Nose

Upper arm

Forearm

Thumb

Second finger

Third finger

WHAT IS A BAT?
Bats are mammals, like elephants, cows, and you! They are the only mammals that can fly. Some bats eat fruit instead of insects. They are called flying foxes. They rely on sight and smell to find their food, rather than echolocation.

The trick of finding food by sound is called echolocation. All the equipment a bat needs is in its head—signals can be sent out either from a bat's mouth or its nose.

ALL ABOUT HUMMINGBIRDS

Hummingbirds are tiny, jewel-like birds . . . and amazing acrobats. They can fly forward, backward, up, and down. They can even hover in one place, like miniature helicopters. This is useful for drinking the sweet nectar hidden deep inside flowers. But it's hard work staying still. The little bird has to beat its wings so quickly they make a humming noise! *Hmmm. . . .*

To hover in one place, the hummingbird has to beat its wings up to 100 times a second. It usually hovers in short bursts with a well-earned rest in between.

Wings

Tail

Hovering uses a lot of energy. The amount of nectar hummingbirds drink in a day to provide this energy is like a person eating 130 loaves of bread!

The hummingbird tips and tilts its tail to keep its balance as it hovers.

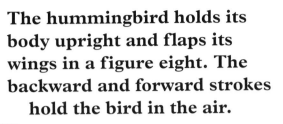

The hummingbird holds its body upright and flaps its wings in a figure eight. The backward and forward strokes hold the bird in the air.

The average-sized hummingbird is about the size of a golf ball.

A long, thin beak and a tongue like a stretched spoon are useful for reaching deep inside flowers to drink nectar.

Hummingbirds have beautiful, colorful feathers that shimmer and shine like precious jewels.

Beak

Tongue

Nectar

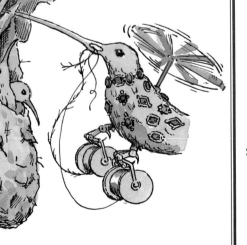

Hummingbirds build tiny, delicate cup-shaped nests from feathers, lichen, grass, and cobwebs. Some fix their nests with leaves, using spider's silk as glue.

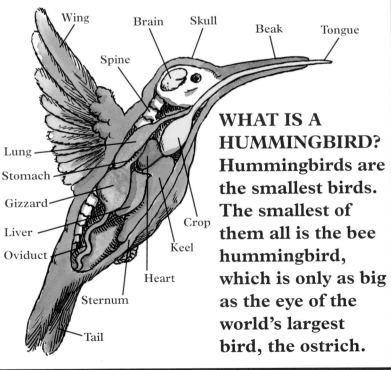

Wing Brain Skull Beak Tongue

Spine

Lung

Stomach

Gizzard

Liver

Oviduct

Crop

Keel

Heart

Sternum

Tail

WHAT IS A HUMMINGBIRD? Hummingbirds are the smallest birds. The smallest of them all is the bee hummingbird, which is only as big as the eye of the world's largest bird, the ostrich.

Giant Atlantic squid

The Atlantic squid has enormous eyes, bigger than dinner plates. They're the largest eyes of any animal.

The sailfish is the fastest fish in the sea. It can zoom along at up to sixty-two miles per hour, faster than a submarine.

AMAZING ANIMALS

Welcome to the Museum of Animal Champions! Stay a while and browse through the record breakers of the animal world—the fastest, biggest, longest, tallest, and smallest. There's a wide range of animals, from a wriggling squid to a tiny frog.

The cheetah is the speediest animal on land. It can sprint at over sixty-two miles per hour. The ostrich is the biggest bird and the fastest runner. At top speed, it can easily beat a racing bike.

Sailfish

Ostrich

Elephant

Cheetah

28

The longest snake is the reticulated python. It is as long as five cars parked in a row.

Reticulated python

Swift

Swift by name, swift by nature! The spine-tailed swift is the fastest bird in the air, speeding along at about 106 miles per hour.

Blue whale

The huge blue whale is the biggest animal ever. Fully grown, it weighs as much as thirty elephants.

Giraffe

Kitti's hog-nose bat

Kitti's hog-nose bat is the smallest mammal. This tiny creature is just over one inch long, about as big as a large bumblebee.

The biggest animal on land is the mighty African elephant. Males weigh about eight tons, as much as sixty pigs!

A male giraffe stands about twenty feet tall. It's the tallest animal on Earth.

The smallest amphibian is a tiny frog called *Sminthillus limbatus*. It is small enough to fit on your fingernail.

Sminthillus limbatus frog

29

INDEX